WELCOME TO
PASSPORT TO READING
A beginning reader's ticket to a brand-new world!

Every book in this program is designed to build read-along and read-alone skills, level by level, through engaging and enriching stories. As the reader turns each page, he or she will become more confident with new vocabulary, sight words, and comprehension.

These PASSPORT TO READING levels will help you choose the perfect book for every reader.

 READING TOGETHER
Read short words in simple sentence structures together to begin a reader's journey.

 READING OUT LOUD
Encourage developing readers to sound out words in more complex stories with simple vocabulary.

 READING INDEPENDENTLY
Newly independent readers gain confidence reading more complex sentences with higher word counts.

 READY TO READ MORE
Readers prepare for chapter books with fewer illustrations and longer paragraphs.

This book features sight words from the educator-supported Dolch Sight Words List. This encourages the reader to recognize commonly used vocabulary words, increasing reading speed and fluency.

For more information, please visit lbyr.com/passporttoreading.

Enjoy the journey!

Little, Brown and Company
Hachette Book Group
1290 Avenue of the Americas, New York, NY 10104
Visit us at LBYR.com

First Edition: August 2022

Little, Brown and Company is a division of Hachette Book Group, Inc.
The Little, Brown name and logo are trademarks of Hachette Book Group, Inc.

The publisher is not responsible for websites (or their content) that are not owned by the publisher.

Library of Congress Control Number: 2020945134

ISBNs: 978-0-316-42935-1 (pbk.), 978-0-316-42934-4 (ebook), 978-0-316-42933-7 (ebook), 978-0-316-42937-5 (ebook)

PRINTED IN CHINA

APS

10 9 8 7 6 5 4 3 2 1

Passport to Reading titles are leveled by independent reviewers applying the standards developed by Irene Fountas and Gay Su Pinnell in *Matching Books to Readers: Using Leveled Books in Guided Reading*, Heinemann, 1999.

Monster Madness!

Adapted by Elle Stephens

LITTLE, BROWN AND COMPANY
New York   Boston

Attention, Miraculous fans!
Look for these words
when you read this book.
Can you spot them all?

monster

pin

slime

instrument

Nino is making a horror movie.
Mylène is the star,
but she is really scared
of the movie's monster!

The monster is just Ivan.

He is wearing a mask.

Mylène is so embarrassed.

Mylène is very sad.
She runs away
and hides in the bathroom.
She wants to be
a better actor.

Hawk Moth can tell
that Mylène is upset.
He sends an evil akuma to her pin.
The akuma turns Mylène into
a villain called the Horrificator!

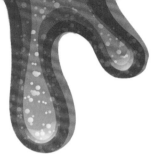

Marinette looks for Mylène
in the bathroom.
The bathroom is empty.
All Marinette finds is
pink slime on a mirror.

Then Marinette hears a scream
and sees even more pink slime.
Oh no!
A student is missing.

A monster is on the loose!
"Tikki, spots on!" Marinette yells.
She turns into a superhero
named Ladybug.

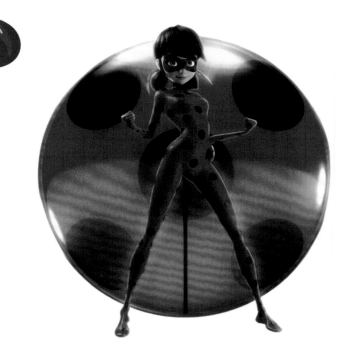

"Plagg, claws out!" Adrien shouts.
He turns into a superhero
named Cat Noir.
Cat Noir and Ladybug
must stop the scary monster.

The Horrificator wants
to scare the students.
It covers the school
in pink slime.

The students are trapped
inside the school!
Their phones do not work.
Oh no!

The Horrificator captures
the students one by one.
The monster gets bigger
when the students are scared.
It gets smaller
when they are not scared.

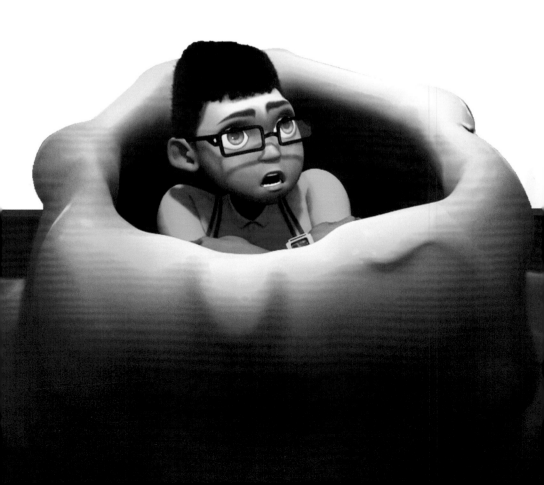

Ladybug and Cat Noir
find the Horrificator
in the classroom.
"Everybody, run!" says Ladybug.

The Horrificator
chases the superheroes.
Ladybug tries to fight
the monster with her yo-yo.
The monster is too strong!

Cat Noir tries to help Ladybug,
but the Horrificator
traps them both in slime!

Then the superheroes break free.
Ladybug has a plan.
"If we defeat fear,
we can defeat the monster!"
she says.

Ladybug and Cat Noir
follow a trail of pink slime.
It leads to the school's basement.

They find all the missing students.
They also find the Horrificator!

"This is getting scary,"
says Ladybug.

She uses her Lucky Charm.
It gives her some guitar strings
and an idea.

Cat Noir uses his Cataclysm.

He breaks some metal bars.

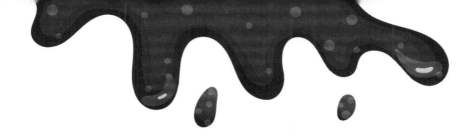

Cat Noir builds a cage.

The Horrificator is trapped!

Ladybug makes each of her classmates an instrument. Together, they play a silly song.

No one is scared anymore! The Horrificator gets smaller and smaller.

Ladybug takes the Horrificator's pin.
She breaks the akuma's spell!
The students are finally free.
All the pink slime is gone.

The Horrificator is gone, too.
Mylène is back to normal!
She is no longer afraid.

It is the perfect ending
to Nino's movie!